ORLANDO'S Home Life.

By Kathleen Hale

Frederick Warne

FREDERICK WARNE

Published by the Penguin Group
27 Wrights Lane, London W8 5TZ, England
Penguin Books USA Inc., 375 Hudson Street, New York, New York 10014, USA
Penguin Books Australia Ltd, Ringwood, Victoria, Australia
Penguin Books Canada Ltd, 2801 John Street, Markham, Ontario, Canada L3R 1B4
Penguin Books (NZ) Ltd, 182-190 Wairau Road, Auckland 10, New Zealand

Penguin Books Ltd, Registered Offices: Harmondsworth, Middlesex, England

First published 1942 by Puffin Books
This revised edition first published 1991 by Frederick Warne & Co. in hardback
and Puffin Books in paperback

10 9 8 7 6 5 4 3 2 1

ISBN 0 7232 3653 4

Printed and bound in Italy by Imago Publishing Limited

Orlando's Home Life.

"It is high time the kittens went to school," said Orlando the Marmalade Cat to his dear wife Grace.

"The fees will be expensive and beyond our means, therefore we must earn the money. I will invent something useful while you make some much-needed object, and we will sell them to the Cats' Shop." (This shop only opens after midnight, and no ordinary human being has ever seen it.

It stocks everything a cat could want, from water-wings to sun-spectacles.)

"I shall miss the kittens terribly," said Grace sadly.

Master fitted up the attic as a workshop for Orlando, who at once invented a "Puss Protector" for fixing under motor-cars to make them jump over jay-walking cats. Meanwhile Grace combed up Master's oldest blankets into nice fluffy new ones for invalid cats.

When Orlando had completed his invention he set to work on a waterproof lotion for spraying cats in wet weather. Then Grace made fur muffs and tippets for travelling cats, with her "Purring Machine" as Tinkle called it.

She kept a set for herself.

They received a lot of money for their work and Orlando was able to send the kittens to school.

Alas! It was not a success . . . the kittens *hated* it, and did all they could to be expelled.

One morning Pansy put the custard-coloured half of her face round the schoolroom door, and the Mistress, not recognizing her, told her to go away. The next day Pansy presented the liquorice-coloured half with the same result.

"That's That!" said Pansy gleefully. "I needn't go to school again!"

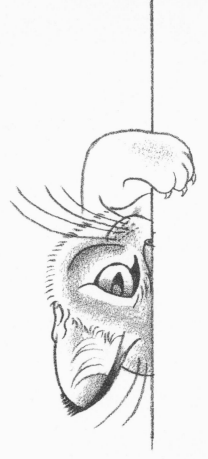

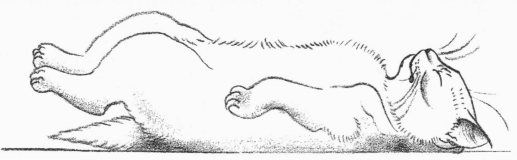

Blanche pretended to faint.

"How pale she is," the Schoolmistress remarked anxiously, and sent her home with one of the big girls when she had recovered.

As for Tinkle, he flipped the ink all over the place with his tail, and untied the school-children's shoelaces.

But what really upset the Mistress was the way he chewed flies in the Poetry Class.

"No more school," Orlando said and Grace was glad for she believed in Mice for cats, not Education.

"But they must learn *something* or nobody will want them," he added.

"Blanche is graceful and could learn dancing," Grace suggested, "and Pansy with her two different faces is well suited to be an Actress."

So every morning Monsieur Pied-à-Terre called and gave Blanche a dancing lesson. And every morning Madame Bouquet taught Pansy how to act.

Tinkle was the real problem. After gravely discussing him, his parents decided that, like some naughty children, he might be Artistic.

"But which will he be good at," inquired Grace, "Painting, Music, Literature or Sculpture?"

"Maybe all four," replied Orlando.

So an Art-Master, Music-Teacher, Professor of Literature and a Sculptor called daily and instructed Tinkle in all the Arts.

Master turned Orlando's workshop into a studio for Tinkle, and Orlando gave him a new paintbox, a harp, a block of wood to carve, and pen and paper.

Poor Tinkle, he got so mixed up that he began carving the harp and painting himself.

Grace had always loved playing with her children, just like a kitten herself; she became very lonely and sad when they were so busy with their lessons.

One day Orlando found her quietly crying into the sink as she washed up.

"My *Dear!*" he exclaimed anxiously. "Whatever is the matter?" After a while she sobbed in reply, "I feel old and ugly."

"Then something must be done at once to prove the contrary," said Orlando firmly. "I'll buy you some fish-and-chips and a frock."

But what pleased Grace most of all - he dismissed all the Professors!

The kittens decided to cheer their mother by acting a play for her. "We have plenty of time now," they said, "in which to make her happy."

A. MacRILL
FRIED FISH & CHIPS

Orlando took Grace to the Fried Fish Shop. They had a slight misunderstanding over the largest piece of fish . . . the only squabble they ever had.

"Excuse me," said Orlando.

"Forgive me," said Grace, "my nerves are on edge."

Off they went to a Mannequin Parade
at the best Costumier's in town.

Instead of a frock Grace chose an imitation
fur coat that looked like leopard skin.

"When I'm tired of myself," she explained,
"I can put it on and pretend I'm someone
else."

"Moddom looks *superb!*" cried the shop
assistant. "A few alterations and the coat
will be ready tomorrow."

"Let's rehearse our play," suggested Tinkle, while Orlando and Grace were out. "The gramophone can be the orchestra," he said, winding it up. "But we must keep everything secret from Mother and talk in Whiskers," and he dusted a record by revolving on it at top speed.

That night Orlando took Grace to buy skates at the Cats' Shop, for he intended to take her to the Skating Rink the following evening.

Orlando's inventions and Grace's blankets and furs were displayed in the shop window, and Mr. Cattermole the shopkeeper welcomed the cats with joy and admiration.

"Your inventions are the talk of the town," he said to Orlando. "They have brought happiness and safety to cats all over the world. Your wife's blankets have saved many a sick cat's life, and her muffs and tippets have set the fashion all over the Continent."

Mr. Cattermole pressed a pair of microphones on them as a token of his esteem.

The following evening Grace's coat arrived; Orlando hailed a taxi and whisked her off to dine at a French restaurant famous for its delicious cooking.

They dined exquisitely on snails and frogs.

Grace looked such a little queen in her lovely furs that all the ladies envied her.

After dinner they went to the
Skating Rink where the orchestra
recognised Orlando, and played
"God Save Our Gracious Cat".
Tingling all over and with
sparkling eyes and frosted whiskers
the elegant cats skated divinely to
the tune of a waltz.

The next day after much washing, manicuring and combing Orlando helped Grace on with her coat and took the family to the Cat Show.

Grace was enchanted by a pair of Siamese kittens and longed for some of her own. Orlando said, "No, we have each other. We don't need any more cats."

Orlando admired a white Persian cat whose owner – a Persian Prince – sat proudly beside her, with all his wives.

The Judge was busy awarding the prizes. Suddenly she saw Grace and was so astonished to see a cat in a fur coat that for a moment she thought it must be a new breed.

On their way home the kittens persuaded Orlando against his better judgement to take them to the Dog Show.

They were only there two minutes . . . the NOISE! and the INSULTS!!!

After breakfast the next morning the kittens rehearsed their play.

Tinkle shut himself up in his studio and made a frightful noise practising the harp.

Pansy arranged the stage and Blanche wrote out the programmes.

The Great Moment arrived and the audience took their seats. Three thumps on the floor by a hind leg behind the scenes announced the beginning, and the curtains were drawn back. Grace read aloud from the programme.

"Scarf Dance by Miss Blanche, Master Tinkle at the Harp." Pansy stood by the gramophone in case Tinkle broke down. He played beautifully however, and Blanche gave a magnificent performance. Their parents were very proud of them.

Scene 2.

Scene 3.

Scene 2 was an impersonation of the "Whiskered Meringue" by Blanche lying curled up on a mirror.

Scene 3, the "Siamese Twins" (to remind Grace of the kittens she liked at the Cat Show). Tinkle with all but his legs, tail and face covered with flour, and Blanche with her legs, tail and face blacked with soot. Both kittens squinted like real Siamese cats.

Scene 4 was the "Hairy Heart" by Tinkle.

Scene 4.

The last scene presented the "Fan Dance" by two mysterious Strangers. First the Lady appeared, and after dancing shyly behind a huge fan she left the stage, and the

Gentleman came on and danced slyly behind *his* huge fan.

Finally they both approached the footlights together—Heavens! the "Pair" was Pansy!

"And now my dear," said Orlando to Grace after the kittens had gone to bed, "what would you like to do?"

"Sing a duet with you on the roof," she replied. "We could use the microphones

Mr. Cattermole gave us."

They sang of Peace and Happiness; the city lay entranced beneath them, and the Moon came out to listen.

Then they went to bed. And after
they had had their bedtime drink of hot
haddock milk, they fell fast asleep.

The End.

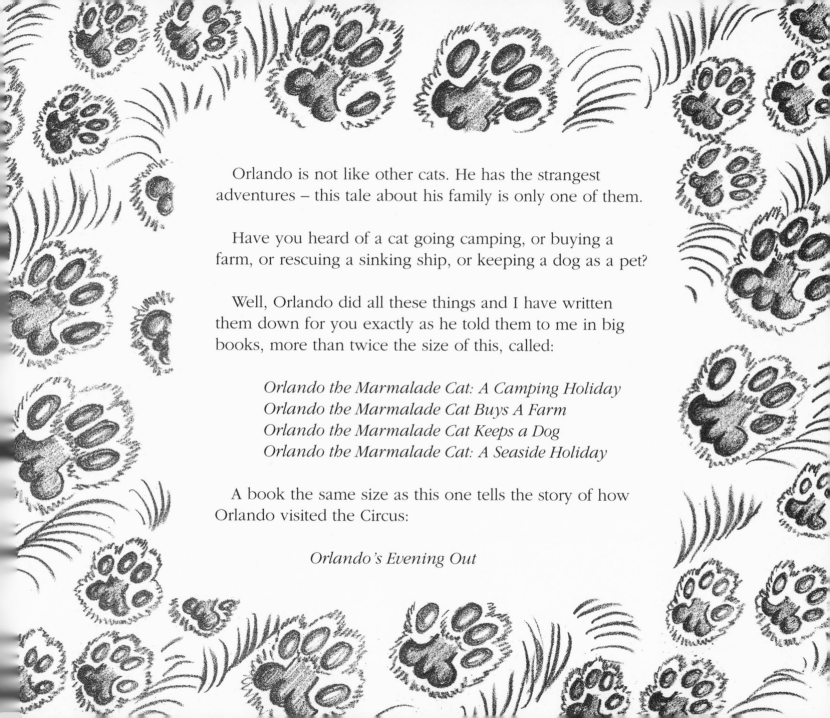

Orlando is not like other cats. He has the strangest adventures – this tale about his family is only one of them.

Have you heard of a cat going camping, or buying a farm, or rescuing a sinking ship, or keeping a dog as a pet?

Well, Orlando did all these things and I have written them down for you exactly as he told them to me in big books, more than twice the size of this, called:

Orlando the Marmalade Cat: A Camping Holiday
Orlando the Marmalade Cat Buys A Farm
Orlando the Marmalade Cat Keeps a Dog
Orlando the Marmalade Cat: A Seaside Holiday

A book the same size as this one tells the story of how Orlando visited the Circus:

Orlando's Evening Out

PUBLISHER'S NOTE

The illustrations in this book were originally drawn directly on to the printing plate by Kathleen Hale and lithographed by W. S. Cowell Ltd, printers of Ipswich. Since no independent artwork remained from this process, the illustrations for this reissue have been scanned from an early edition which was checked and corrected by the author.

Orlando's Home Life was first published in 1942 during the Second World War, and the restrictions imposed by the severe paper shortage at that time were reflected in the book's cramped design. For the 1991 edition, therefore, the text has been reset in a more spacious layout, the page size increased to give expanded margins and a separate title page added. The book appears for the first time in an open format and design that entirely accords with the author's wishes and original intentions.